What's Making Walter C. Laugh?

Ginny Jordan

ISBN: 978-1-4834-6463-3 (sc)
ISBN: 978-1-4834-6462-6 (hc)
ISBN: 978-1-4834-6464-0 (e)

Library of Congress Control Number: 2017901036

Lulu Publishing Services rev. date: 2/28/2017

This book belongs to

_____

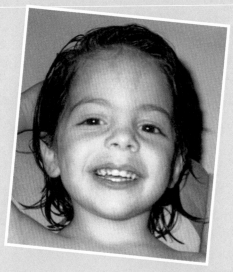

This book is dedicated to
everyone who laughed with
C. and to everyone who
laughs with this book.

Acknowledgments

Thank you to all my editors. You know who you are. Walter C. is because of you. I am who I am because of you. You are the smiles in my heart and in my life. *What's Making Walter C. Laugh?* is as much yours as it is mine. My thank you, like my love for you, is as big as the sky.

Have fun!

What's making
Walter C. laugh?

Is it a penguin flying
upside-down in the sky?

Is it unicorns riding unicycles juggling ice-cream cones?

Is it a kangaroo running backward flying a kite?

Is it a monkey skateboarding down the sidewalk?

Is it a goldfish dancing with a banana on the kitchen table?

Is it three dolphins wearing straw hats riding a bicycle built for three?

No, it's not a penguin, or unicorns, or a kangaroo, or a monkey, or a goldfish, or dolphins.

Is it a snowman eating pizza in the bathtub?

Is it a parade of cupcakes
marching down the street?

Is it a giraffe cooking pancakes?

Is it a ladybug ice-skating on a Popsicle?

Is it an octopus playing goalie in a soccer game?

No, it's not a snowman, or a parade of cupcakes, or a frog,

or a giraffe, or a ladybug, or an octopus.

What do you think is
making Walter C. laugh?

These blank pages are for you to draw what you think is making Walter C. laugh.

Have fun!

Made in the USA
Middletown, DE
04 April 2018